The Pelican Hotel

Jacey Bici

Published by JCBC Publishing, LLC 2026

Cover Design by GetCovers

All the characters in this book are fictitious, and any resemblance to actual persons living or dead is purely coincidental.

All inquiries should be directed to

JCBC Publishing, LLC

14621 E SR 70 #247

Lakewood Ranch, FL 34202

ISBN-13: **978-1-969160-05-9**

One

I moved between my world of champagne clinking in crystal flutes and his world of dirty gym clothes piled in the corner of a shabby apartment. Acting as though I could keep the two separate, I had spent the last two years sailing by.

A doctor by trade, I filled my days in the hospital doing what doctors do. I won't list those things here, for fear of dying of boredom, but suffice it to say from sun up to sun down I busied myself patching up humans. It had been my dream, and most days it felt like enough.

But at Ocean Hospital, I was the outsider. I had come from New York, I was single and as far as I knew, no one else was a blend of Palestinian and Puerto Rican. Maybe they were only constructs I created, but the otherness had left me searching for more.

Ever since I found the man I call Tallahassee, another place was beginning to feel like home. An hour away, or maybe a lifetime, I was untethered. In his tiny apartment near the Florida State campus, I traded the stethoscopes and pagers that had once delighted me for gentle mornings and the easy warmth of his embrace. There, I wasn't Dr. Nassrin Fahadi. I was just me.

I rolled out from beneath Tallahassee's arm, planting a soft kiss on his forehead without waking him. The aroma of brewing coffee wafted in through the window from the nearby cafes, but he would sleep through it, blissfully unaware of a world that might devour him whole. Unlike the students rising early for coffee, he was a bartender. Having spent the night serving cheap beer to twenty-somethings dancing and sloshing their drinks as they yelled over the music, and serving Manhattans to me folded up in a corner, he wouldn't be up for espresso anytime soon.

Tallahassee was the key to my lock. I could breathe around him--let my hair down. I could be myself and that was enough. That notion alone propelled me to his kitchen where I pulled down the drip coffee maker and four mugs.

His parents were arriving soon. According to him, meeting his mother was monumental. She meant the world to him.

The charming campus brimmed with youth that felt like a chasm between his life and mine. I glanced out the window, catching a hipster couple curling waxed mustaches, tattoos rising up their legs from holy shoes.

I heard him stir in bed and when I returned, he was awake, sitting up, his messy blond hair and bare chest calling to me. I abandoned the coffee as he coaxed me back to bed. Ignoring the gnawing emptiness in my stomach, I wrapped my legs around him, drinking him in like an elixir. The world outside faded as he cradled my head in one hand, his eyes locked on mine—an intimate expression that transcended mere lust. I loved him.

A knock at the door sent us hopping into jeans and buttoning shirts. His parents were early. Bob and Dotty Newsome were lovely; she bubbled over with southern charm while he shook his son's hand heartily before dropping into a chair.

"Mom, Dad--this is Nassrin,"he said, as his mother pulled me into a hug, spilling coffee onto the floor. Her questions came fast—about the hospital, my work, the mole on her back —until my phone interrupted, vibrating insistently with the hospital's demands. I silenced it, smiling through the noise.

"So, how did you two meet?" asked his father.

Before either of us could explain the chance encounter at the bar, my phone rang again. It was Karen, one of the new doctors at the hospital.

"It's alright," they assured me. "Take your call."

I stepped into the kitchen.

"Did you hear?" asked Karen.

"Hear what?"

"Dr. Aberdeen is hosting a dinner at The Pelican."

"Should that mean something to me?" I asked.

"Yes!" exclaimed Karen. "The Pelican Hotel is the only nice place in Gilbert. It's right on the beach and it used to be a mobster mansion and it's six-stories high and--"

"Karen, I have to go," I interrupted, straining to hear what they were saying about me in the next room.

"Just wait," she replied. "Dr. Aberdeen has a big announcement. Next Saturday."

"Okay. Talk to you later." My finger hovered to end the call. I was catching wisps of conversation floating in from the sofa.

Are you eating enough? Look at the dust on this table! You need to dust. Nassrin seems nice. I can't believe my son found a real doctor!

"Wait!" Karen exclaimed. "I need you to cover my shift this afternoon. I'm going to the mall to get a dress ."

"I'm in Tallahassee," I replied with a laugh.

"You could be here in an hour," she countered.

"I'm hanging up."

"Okay," Karen relented. "It's going to be so sad when you need someone to cover *you*..."

Ending the call, I slipped the phone into my pocket and returned to the living room. As Tallahassee offered around the tray of desserts I had picked up from the Middle Eastern bakery on Appalachee Parkway, his mother peppered me with questions.

"Was that the hospital, honey?" his mother asked.

"Yes. Yes it was, but it was nothing important."

"Do you work in the emergency room?"

"Nope. I'm the doctor for the admitted patients."

"Oh, I bet you see some really interesting cases. What's the craziest thing you've ever seen?"

As I racked my brain, skipping quickly past the top three cases in search of something polite (the top three being a battery where it didn't belong, a set of eviscerated intestines and a self-inflicted bow-and-arrow mishap), my phone began vibrating again. I held up a finger as I pulled out the phone and glanced at the text.

"A guy with a bow and arrow mishap," I mumbled as I read Karen's new message.

> I found someone to cover my shift. But just so you know, if you insist on slumming with your bartender boyfriend instead of helping your colleagues, you'll never get anywhere in Doctors Inc.

I knitted my brow; Tallahassee rested a hand on my shoulder. I could see his eyes on the text. "She's new," I explained. "She's stupid. Don't worry about her."

But Doctors Inc. had succeeded in dismantling the vital meeting with his parents. His parents didn't want to keep me from my work, so we said our goodbyes and they left in a flurry of hugs and reminders to vacuum the apartment.

"Your mom is really nice. I'm sorry work got in the way," I said when we were alone. I wrapped my arms around his waist, and he kissed my head. Just as I exhaled, thoughts of the bedroom on my mind, my phone started again. "I'll put it in airplane mode," I said into his chest.

He reached a hand into my pocket and handed me the phone. I winced at the name on the text.

Dr. Aberdeen:

> I'm pulling you to cover the rest of Karen's shift this afternoon. There's an emergency with her cat.

I jammed the phone face down on an end table. Like a cornered animal, I curled myself helplessly onto the end of the sofa.

"Can I ask you something?" Tallahassee said, looking serious.

I nodded, tensing even more. "Sure."

"My friend wants me to go to the boxing gym with him today," he admitted, his voice tentative.

I let out a breath of relief, my face breaking into a smile. "I thought you were going to break my heart for a minute there!"

He laughed and took my hand in his. "I will never break your heart. Unless you're mad about the boxing."

I grinned and pointed at my phone. "I guess I'm needed in Gilbert today anyway."

I paused, growing serious. The corporate nonsense had become too much. Why should I miss out on this man I loved to cover a fake cat emergency?

"I think I'm going to resign."

"Nassrin!" he exclaimed. "You love being a doctor!"

"I did, yeah. I got to do a lot of cool stuff, but it's too

much. And what's next? Having a family that I get to abandon for the next thousand patients?"

He let out a breath. "What are you going to do?"

"We could live off my sign-on bonus until you finish law school."

He nodded. I bit my lip. It was the most serious conversation we had ever had, but the moment felt right. "Sure, Nassrin," he replied.

He had helped me pack my bag. At the car, he kissed me softly, warmth radiating between us as he opened my door. I cupped his cheeks, kissing him fiercely, the urge to stay overwhelming. Tossing my bag onto the passenger seat, I drove away, heart heavy yet buoyed by the hope of a new future.

It didn't seem possible this day had come. Me—Nassrin Fahadi—who as a child wore a toy stethoscope around my neck like other girls wore costume jewelry. Me who dreamed of saving lives and sacrificed my twenties for the inside of a hospital ward was now rehearsing my resignation.

The Pelican Hotel, its majesty a metaphor for the life I was giving up, would make the perfect setting. The approaching day loomed like an apparition in the dark.

Two

The week passed uneventfully, and then I found myself in The Pelican Hotel dining hall surrounded by the group of doctors I had once clambered to be like. But tonight, under the chandeliers, I felt like a stranger in my own life. The other doctors celebrated, but I was only there to say goodbye. No more dreaming. It was time for action.

In the moment before my magnanimous resignation from Doctors Inc, an old woman, Dr. Aberdeen's wife, prepared to squelch my dreams. She eyed me from across the dining table, her sights set on me. But before she could engage me in conversation, I slipped away to the ladies' room to find a quiet place to rehearse.

Facing the mirror, I began the rehearsal. "I've met a man, and I know this sounds crazy, but I've changed my mind about being a doctor." I sipped from the crystal tumbler I held in my hand, the whiskey burning the back of my throat. *Too sincere. No one needs to know I'm crazy. Try again.*

"The new doctors you hired—they're no good at all. One is a narcissist and the other is a hair brain." *True*, I mused. *But let's not make this about them. Try again.*

"Dr. Aberdeen." This time, I met my reflection's eyes and frowned. The whiskey I had imbibed made its way to my head, a soft blanket of courage. "Thank you for the opportunity to work at the lovely Ocean Hospital, but I'm heading in a new direction."

I shook my head. My words were coming out slurred to the point of ridiculous. *Vapid and rehearsed.* "Just say it!" I shouted at my reflection.

Throwing my head back, I downed the rest of the whiskey. As my eyes scanned the vacant space, I reassured myself that any guttural sounds would be silenced by the luxurious velvet covering the walls. *Again.*

"Dr. Aberdeen, I hate you and I hate your stupid hospital! Your company is a beast. Your new doctors stink, your leadership is terrible, and I quit!" I shouted, surprising myself with the force of my voice.

The door burst open, and the one person who could destroy my plans stumbled in, arms laden with a bulky box.

"How much did you hear?" I grimaced through hands that had flown to my mouth. I peered down at the old woman, Dr. Aberdeen's wife. Her thin lips twisted in disapproval.

"It would be a shame to quit now, dear," said Isabelle Aberdeen. Her tone was rich with authority. "Open the box."

"Isabelle, I can explain." I grabbed the counter to steady myself.

Isabelle waved me off with a flick of her wrist. "What is his name?" she asked.

"What do you mean?"

"You said, 'I've met a man, and I know this sounds crazy.'" Isabelle made air quotes with knobby knuckles.

I hesitated, my resolve wavering. "He's no one," I answered as I knelt and pulled back the box's flap, curiosity getting the best of me. "How did you find me?"

"I just followed the echoes of your impassioned speech," Isabelle replied, pointing to a glossy magazine stacked in the box. "Hand me one of those, would you?"

"What is this?" I asked, passing over a magazine from the top of a large stack. My mind still raced with daydreams of resignation.

"*Le Crème*," Isabelle announced, the magazine's title rolling off her tongue with an elegant flair.

"About what you heard," I began, determined to steer the conversation back to the awful words I uttered about Isabelle's husband. But Isabelle's hand rose to silence me.

"Nassrin, dear, you must be wondering why I tracked you down in the ladies' room with a box of magazines."

True enough, just ten minutes ago, Isabelle was chirping commands to The Pelican waitstaff, indifferent to my existence. "Why?" I asked.

"*Le Crème* is writing a feature on Doctors Inc." Isabelle grasped my wrist. I flinched, startled by the woman's strength. "Dr. Aberdeen is about to announce it; he's going to name one of you the medical director, and *Le Crème* is going to cover it."

I chuckled and yanked my wrist, almost wrestling free before Isabelle could finish. Lotions and perfumes filled ceramic vessels, swimming before my eyes as I imagined something far away. I wasn't interested in being the medical director. I was on the verge of walking away from it all. Love, even in a crappy college apartment, was worth more to me than all of this. Maybe if Ocean Hospital wasn't complicated by conniving coworkers and a terrible boss. But it was, and I had to choose.

Isabelle's grip tightened around my wrist, urgency sparkling in her gaze. "Dr. Aberdeen will select one of you at the Christmas party next week, and the lucky doctor will be in a photoshoot with me."

It was shocking how far off the mark Isabelle had flung her pitch. I reached a hand behind my back and unfastened the hook that held my evening gown around my neck, allowing my gown to slump over one shoulder. The stuffy evening needed some breathing room. Grasping the clip that held my hair, the long black mane came tumbling down. "I don't want to be a supervisor, Isabelle. I want to be a homemaker."

Isabelle was unfazed. She flipped through her copy of *Le Crème* with nonchalance, pausing here and there on the pages with beautiful photos of the town. "You can't quit now, dear. I want you on the cover."

I studied my reflection in the mirror, never having considered myself the cover girl type. "Why?"

"Diversity," she replied.

I touched my hair, considering for just a moment how I would look on the cover. But I didn't believe Isabelle any more than I believed that Karen's cat was prone to emergencies. "Tom is black, and Alex is Chinese," I replied. "Why me?"

Instead of answering, Isabelle handed me a magazine, her expression unreadable. Could it be that the Aberdeens truly believed I was perfect—not just for the cover, but as a doctor, too?

I blinked, lifting the magazine from Isabelle's hand. The card stock was heavy, as rich as the photograph on that month's cover. I traced a finger over the image of The Pelican, the grand hotel where I now stood, perched on the shore of the Gulf of Mexico. *Le Crème* was someone else's life. My dreams were always about the patients. Never the accoutrements. I slid the magazine across the counter, shaking my head.

"You'll lose your sign-on bonus if you resign," Isabelle snapped, her voice suddenly sharp. "Did you think you were going to live on that?"

I choked, alarmed at the shift in Isabelle's tone and

surprised by her accuracy. Was that true? I hadn't considered the possibility of losing my nest egg. I coughed, finding myself unable to clear my throat. It didn't matter. I didn't need the money. He would take care of me.

I filled my empty glass with water from the tap. As I gulped the tepid water, my throat now calm, a text sent a tremor through my phone which lay on the counter. It was him.

Don't resign yet!

Isabelle dropped the magazine and snatched up my phone in one swift motion. I lunged for it, but the old woman was surprisingly quick.

"We're past the point of secrets, Dr. Fahadi," she said as she squinted at the phone.

"Don't resign yet!" Isabelle read from the screen. "*We need to talk.*" She turned the screen to me. "Who is this? It just says 'Tallahassee.'"

I coughed again, my throat tight. Confusion, anger, shame--they each swirled like a bad omen.

Was he having second thoughts? Was I? Who dedicates their life to being a doctor just to walk away at the first sign of a cute boy? *Don't resign yet*--what did that mean?

"He's no one," I replied, grabbing my phone. If I could tell the Aberdeens I was resigning, why was it so hard to talk about my boyfriend?

My pride was seeping into places it didn't belong and getting in the way. He wasn't no one. He was *the one*. But instead of conjuring images of wedding bells, as soon as he challenged my resignation, I found myself stuck on the details. His tattered clothes, his run-down apartment. Was I foolish to put my fate in his hands? I thought he was a good investment, but as I glanced at *Le Crème*, my cheeks burned.

I'm pulling up out front.

I softened. Maybe there was a simple explanation.

Isabelle hoisted up her box. “I don’t like these ideas he’s planting in your head, Nassrin. Your career is not a game you can just walk away from. You spent your life building this.”

I waved my phone through the air in agreement. “He told me not to resign. It doesn’t look like I’m going anywhere.”

I was back where I started, fighting against the career that I created.

As Isabelle pressed her back into the door, a motherly tone took over. “Do you want to resign or not?"

I bit my lip. “Not anymore. No.”

“I don’t want to see you with that guy, Nassrin. He's going to be the death of your career.”

I had worked for Doctors Inc. long enough not to trust anyone with the last name Aberdeen. “Or is it that you want to keep me focused on making money for Ocean Hospital?”

Isabelle rolled her eyes, but she didn't deny it. "If you decide to choose ‘Tallahassee’ over Doctors Inc., I’ll be delighted to speak to my husband about your little tantrum. He will fire you.”

THREE

BEFORE ANYONE OF CONSEQUENCE CAUGHT SIGHT OF the man I called Tallahassee, I rushed outside to intercept him, tripping over my skirt in my haste. It wasn't just that I didn't want my colleagues to see me with him; I didn't want anyone to see me with him—not here, not now. For two years, I'd kept him tucked away in another town, safely out of sight. What would they think?

Nassrin, he's so... young. So carefree. So... unlike you.

Isabelle had practically said it outright. He was the reason I'd been willing to risk everything, to walk away from a career I'd spent my life building. But now that plan was dead, and the thought of introducing him to my polished, high-stakes world at this moment—when I was already faltering—was too much to bear.

The Dodge Neon idled in the valet line a few cars back, conspicuous with its rust and rumbles. I waved to Tallahassee, longing to share with him everything that just took place with Isabelle. At the same time, I wondered about my empty chair at the Aberdeen's gathering.

Tallahassee climbed out of the Dodge Neon, handing his keys to an attendant wearing much finer clothes than he did.

I flinched. His face looked wrong. A swollen asymmetry plagued his left eye, a flourish of crimson taking over his lid. Had he been stung by a wasp? Was he here for medical attention?

"What happened?" I exclaimed as he wrapped me in an embrace. For a moment, I forgot about our broken plans and the danger of being seen with him, and I wrapped my arms around him, too.

Couples in suits and heels stepped around us as their gleaming cars were whisked away. The valet staff were in constant motion opening doors, tossing keys and jogging to the lot. Money changed hands. All the while Tallahassee stood open-mouthed without reply.

"I didn't realize The Pelican was so big," he remarked after some time. I followed his gaze as it swept over the giant portico, the stucco walls and terracotta tiles on the roof high above.

I pulled him to the side and touched his swollen eye with a gentle finger. "What happened?"

"Did you resign yet, Nassrin?" His tone was urgent, and he moved my hand away from his face.

"No!" I cried impatiently. "What's going on with you?"

"There's something I need to tell you," he confessed.

My eyes darted around us. My evening gown and spiked heels were at odds with his ripped tank top and jeans. *This is who inspired me to start my life over?* A sliver of doubt crept in not for the first time that evening. "Come with me," I said. "I have a room here tonight."

I sucked in a breath, then took him by the hand. We marched through a hallway where servers burst in and out of swinging doors. We weaved through trays of food and drinks until we reached the stairwell. The sound of the door slamming as I barreled through echoed up the stairs.

"Where are you taking me?" Tallahassee asked as he trailed behind. The scent of cigarettes was strong, and a waiter perched on the stairs blew a plume of smoke and nodded at us as we climbed past.

"We're almost there," I promised.

In the room was a bed with a velour cover and matching sofa. The furniture disappeared into the gold trim and dark walls. All of it was there to frame the balcony, which created a portrait of the sea. The black of night smudged out the view, but the sound of the waves crashing into the beach remained. "You should see it in the morning," I told him. The quiet of the room settled my anxious heart as I stole a glance in his direction.

Tallahassee stepped around me and swung open the sliding glass door. The waves crashed loudly, and the breeze picked up a strand of my hair. It set the strand dancing in playful circles. Whatever he was going to tell me, I sensed it would be alright because he was there, and I did love him, after all.

"I got kicked out of law school," he whispered.

My eyes grew wide, and my heart squeezed with rising panic. No wonder he didn't want me to quit my job and come crawling to him. This was not part of the plan, his being expelled. This would not do at all. I folded my arms over my chest.

"What happened?" I asked for the third time.

Tallahassee pushed a thumb into his eye as if putting his face back together would fix what had broken. *Our dreams*, I thought. "My sparring partner clipped my face. It was an accident," he explained.

I held myself tightly, not understanding. "All this over a boxing gym?"

"I wasn't supposed to come back to court with black eye. Three strikes--I'm out."

"The dean won't take an apology letter instead?" I asked. His silence was answer enough. I had so many questions and yet there was nothing to say. I let him lead me to the couch where I leaned my head on his shoulder. "I was going to get out," I whispered, my gaze fixed on the wall.

"I'm sorry, Nassrin."

"I can't quit now. I can't default on my loans."

"I'll keep tending bar for now," he whispered.

"Ocean Hospital is going to eat me alive."

"I could burn it down for you," he offered.

I laughed despite the lump in my throat. "You saw them pull me in so Karen could go shopping. They're just going to keep coming for me."

"You'll get to save a hundred thousand lives while I work my way back," he said, squeezing my hand.

"We were going to have a simple life. We were going to build a home."

"We will," he promised.

I wrapped a strand of hair around my finger and watched the spiral unravel as I pulled my hand away. I should tell him that Isabelle didn't want me seeing him. He should understand why he needed to stay hidden for me to keep my job. But something held me back. My pride, probably. Because it wasn't like I wanted to punish him for unraveling things, exactly. It was just that I had the upper hand. He didn't know Isabelle overheard me blasting Dr. Aberdeen. As far as he knew, this was all because of his black eye. Let him think that.

"Isabelle said they're planning to choose one of us to be the medical director."

"That could be a good thing," he said tentatively.

"It can't be me," I replied. "It has to be Tom Rogers."

I turned to him. I wanted anger, but only sadness came. I

ached for Tallahassee, but I was also a bit relieved. Relieved that Isabelle hadn't thrown me away after what she overheard. Still, I should get to Dr. Aberdeen before Isabelle did. "I better get back to dinner," I added. "Stay here and put some ice on that thing."

Four

Across the grand ballroom of the magnificent Pelican Hotel, I could see the dining hall—equally as impressive but far more intimidating. With Tallahassee tucked safely in my hotel room, there was still time to slip back to dinner before the main course was served. My fate lay there, in the hands of Isabelle Aberdeen, the old crone who could single handedly end my career. I'd made sure she heard my dissatisfaction loud and clear. If I had any hope of salvaging my future, I needed to get to the giant among men who ran Doctors Inc., Ronald Aberdeen.

And yes, he was a giant—towering over the average man in both stature and success. Just thinking about facing him made my heart thunder. In fact, it might just explode during the conversation I was about to have. Most of my interactions with him had been mercifully electronic. I could still remember the sting of one of his passive-aggressive emails: *Dear team, stop calling consultants at all hours of the night. You should be competent enough to take care of things on your own.*

That had been for me. A patient with appendicitis. I wasn't a surgeon—how the hell was I supposed to handle that? Surgeons, in my opinion, were trolls, traumatized and incapable of normal human interaction. Aberdeen himself had been a surgeon before becoming the company president. *Once a surgeon, always a surgeon,* I thought bitterly as I hurried toward the dining hall. What was I going to say? Was it already too late?

The atrium buzzed with the mingling of staff and the well-dressed dinner crowd, and The Pelican's restored opulence felt like a relic of another world. As I passed a seaside balcony, the winter breeze caught my scarf and fluttered it around my shoulders like an anxious whisper. My heels clicked against the checkerboard tiles, faster and faster, as I approached the dining hall. For a moment, I let my eyes wander to the terrace. The ocean lapped gently below, and couples dotted the balcony, laughing and carefree. One woman stood out to me—bold and delighted with the evening. I imagined being her for a second. *Go talk to him,* I ordered myself.

But then someone called out from the bar.

It was Opal Collins, the other newly hired doctor. Of course, it was Opal. The nitwit could barely finish her work at Ocean Hospital, let alone a beer at The Pelican. And here she was, slowing me down again.

"I can't sit and chat, Opal," I said sharply. "I have to find Dr. Aberdeen."

"He's in there," she said, pointing toward the kitchen. "Making sure the cooks get the salad right. Sit at the bar with me; you'll see him come out."

"Oh," I replied, looking for an excuse to follow Aberdeen into the kitchen. "I better go let them know I'm allergic to pork."

"I ordered you a vegetarian plate," Opal whispered, dabbing at something on her dress.

I sighed and then relented, reluctantly climbing onto the barstool beside her.

"So, how do you like living here in Gilbert?" I asked, trying not to sound annoyed.

Opal laughed. "I grew up here. And it's pronounced *zheel-bair*. It's French."

I tilted my head. "I thought it was Gill-Bert."

"Anyone who didn't grow up here calls it Gill-Bert," she chuckled. "I take it you're not originally from here?"

"You don't see a lot of Fahadis in *zheel-bair*," I said with a wry smile. "I'm from New York."

Opal nodded. "And your heritage?"

"Palestine," I replied. I wanted to dislike her, but her kindness was unnervingly contagious.

"Native American," she said proudly, pointing to herself.

"Why aren't you with the others?" I asked.

She nodded to her chest where two dark, wet spots on her dress revealed the answer. Not spilt beer, but mother's milk. I felt a pang of guilt for my earlier irritation.

"Children?" I asked.

"Two," she said. "Apparently, the little one is ready for dinner."

Without thinking, I pulled my scarf from my shoulders. "Take this," I said, draping it around her neck. I adjusted it to cover the wet spots. "Can I ask you something?"

"Sure," she said, finishing her beer.

"Have you ever thought about staying home instead?" My eyes flitted back to the kitchen door, still no sign of Dr. Aberdeen. The wait staff buzzed around like bees in a hive.

"Every working woman thinks about it," she said with a shrug.

"Why not do it? Why not quit?"

"I like the patients too much," she said simply, her eyes sparkling.

"Really? Even old man Knickerbocker who always tries to flirt with us?"

Opal smirked. "Yeah, that guy's my favorite."

I hated to admit it, but the nitwit was right. The patients were the glue holding me together under the weight of corporate demands. Each one brought a unique story, a pearl that I added to my string. No other life would afford me the opportunity to encounter their precious, vulnerable, incredible stories.

"I'm impressed that you can do it all." I relaxed, realizing that if I stayed at Ocean Hospital, it meant gaining a friendship with the nitwit, who wasn't so bad after all.

"Do what all?" Opal asked.

"Everything. Doctor. Wife. Mother."

"Oh, I don't do any of it well," she laughed, brushing me off.

"Huh," I replied, my mouth falling open slightly as I considered this. The thought of doing anything half-way hadn't entered my mind.

Then Opal pointed across the room. "There he is."

My heart leapt. Dr. Aberdeen had just stepped out of the kitchen. I launched off the barstool so quickly I nearly twisted an ankle. But just as I spotted him, another figure stepped into my path.

Tallahassee.

I groaned audibly, wishing I had made it clear that he was supposed to stay in the room. The mangled idiot was wearing a sports coat—clearly borrowed from The Pelican. *This cannot be happening.*

"Tallahassee!" I exclaimed. "What are you doing?"

"I came to be the muscle," he said lightly. "If your boss is as tough as you say, you might need backup."

"Go sit with Opal," I snapped, frustration bubbling over. "And stay out of sight. That black eye got you tossed out of law school. Let's not get tossed out of The Pelican."

Opal, to my surprise, was laughing. "What happened to his face? And why do you call him Tallahassee?"

"So she doesn't confuse me with Gainesville!" he said, grinning. They both broke into giggles while I stood there, eyebrows raised. How was this funny?

Tallahassee did what I asked and took the barstool beside Opal. When I turned back to look for Aberdeen, he was gone.

"Okay, guys," I said, standing before them and gripping their shoulders. "What are we going to do? I might have said some things about Ronald Aberdeen, and Isabelle might have heard them. How do I fix this?"

"Get Isabelle," Opal said, pointing across the room. Sure enough, the old crone had just stepped out of the kitchen.

"That's it!" I said, rushing toward Isabelle. I turned back to the bar as I trotted away. "Tallahassee, keep your head down. You look hideous."

I winked, and to my surprise—and slight irritation—he beamed.

FIVE

JUST AS ISABELLE REACHED FOR THE DOOR TO THE dinner party, the weight of my entire future pressing down on me, I acted without thinking.

"Isabelle!" I called out, my voice sharper than I intended. She froze mid-step, turning to face me. I leaned in, lowering my voice so only she could hear. "Can we talk privately?"

"Of course, dear," Isabelle said, dabbing her face with a tissue. She turned away from the dining hall, and I led her to a heavy door nearby. Pushing it open, I found an empty ballroom, dimly lit by massive chandeliers turned down low. Rows of chairs filled the space, standing like silent witnesses, and the air was cold and stale. I shivered but pressed forward, determination swelling in my chest.

"We have to talk about what happened," I said, my voice firm, though my fingers trembled slightly as I brushed the velvet floral pattern on a seat cushion.

"They use this room for funerals," Isabelle replied absently, lowering herself gracefully into one of the chairs.

"If you tell Dr. Aberdeen what I said about him, you'll

need this room for *my* funeral," I quipped, trying to break the tension.

Her lips curved ever so slightly, a knowing smirk that made it clear she held all the cards. "I'll require something in return."

"You want me to do the photoshoot." I traced the cushion nervously, already knowing where this was headed.

"And medical director," she added, her tone as unyielding as the walls around us.

I shut my eyes tightly, trying to block out the suffocating weight of her demand. Someone else could do it. Anyone else. I imagined acting as Dr. Aberdeen's right-hand man, always at his beck and call--responsible not only for patients' wellbeing, but for the health of Doctors Inc. as well. I didn't want more responsibility; I just wanted to bide my time until Tallahassee could support us. A simple life. That's all I wanted.

"Why me?" I asked.

"You'll make a great director," she replied. "And it will be good for your career. You want it all--a career and a family--this will help get you there. Eventually."

"Tom can do it," I offered quickly. Tom Rogers was the logical choice—the veteran doctor, the father figure. He was steady, experienced, and already in the dining room with the others.

"It won't be Tom," Isabelle said, her voice dropping into a conspiratorial tone. "Ronald made that clear to me."

"Tom is the obvious choice!" I exclaimed, fighting to steady my voice even as my stomach clenched. "Tom will protect us." The words hung heavy in the air, laden with truth I couldn't take back. Tom would protect us, not from outside threats, but from the Aberdeens themselves.

Isabelle's nostril's flared, her understanding of my insinuation clear on her face. "Nassrin, you can't keep saying things like that!"

I flinched, realizing I was losing ground. "I didn't mean it," I mumbled, trying to recover.

"Please, dear," Isabelle said, her voice softening but her grip on my future tightening. "I know who my husband is. I know he's difficult, and that scares you. Ronald wants Karen to be the medical director."

My eyes widened. "Karen Chamberlain? The *new* doctor who finds more ways to get out of work than a magician pulls rabbits out of hats?" The words tumbled out before I could stop them.

Karen was useless. She was the kind of person who booked dinner reservations instead of finishing her tasks. Worse, she had a knack for gaslighting anyone who called her out.

Hang in there, girl. You got this.

Don't let this job overwhelm you.

Or the classic: *I can't work nights. My cats are on a feeding schedule.*

"Nassrin!" Isabelle's voice snapped me out of my downward spiral. She grabbed my wrist, her delicate bony fingers surprisingly strong. "That's why it has to be you."

I felt trapped in her web. Sighing deeply, I said, "Give me tonight to consider it."

Her smile widened into a Cheshire grin. "I can wait. But tomorrow, I tell Dr. Aberdeen everything you said about him."

I groaned inwardly.

"We've been away too long. The dinner party is waiting." Isabelle said. "Let's get back so Dr. Aberdeen can announce the photoshoot and the search for the new medical director." With that, Isabelle pulled open the heavy door as though it weighed nothing. She wasn't as frail as she seemed.

Back in the dining room, the scene was almost surreal. The table loomed large, my colleagues seated around it in a lavish display. A fresh cocktail waited for me at my seat, sparkling in its crystal glass. Laughter and quiet conversation mingled under the soft glow of the chandelier.

Isabelle beamed at Dr. Aberdeen, who sat at the table's head. If she planned to betray me, she showed no sign of it now.

I had barely slipped back into my chair when Dr. Aberdeen rose, tapping his fork against his glass. The soft chime silenced the room. Isabelle nodded at me, her casual smile a silent reminder: *Do what I ask, and your secret is safe.*

Next to me, Opal froze mid-spoonful, a drop of lobster bisque splashing onto the scarf I'd lent her. I cringed, handing her a napkin before turning my attention back to Dr. Aberdeen.

"I took over Sunshine Medical and transformed it into Doctors Inc years ago," he began, his voice commanding the room. I couldn't help but glance at Karen. She was seated on his other side, her face lit with giddy anticipation. How had *she* gotten that seat? And did she know there was a splotch of purple lipstick on her front tooth?

"Since then, I'm proud to say we've flourished," Ronald continued, flashing a smile at Isabelle. "Thanks to you all, we are now the largest group on the Gulf Coast."

Isabelle pulled a copy of *Le Crème* from a box and stood beside him as he continued. "In one week, *Le Crème* will be here at The Pelican."

As Ronald spoke, I scanned the table. Alex sat quietly on my other side, while Tom, across from me, wore an expression of boredom. He had no idea what was coming. Of course he didn't. He wasn't the one shouting resignation plans across the hotel.

"At our annual Christmas party, we will choose one of you to join Isabelle in a photoshoot to be featured on the cover of *Le Crème*. And I'm promoting that person to be our first-ever medical director."

Excitement rippled through the group, but dread coiled tighter around my chest. Would I even have a job tomorrow? Karen clapped her hands like a child on Christmas morning. Opal fumbled with the soup stain on the scarf. I twirled a piece of hair around my finger, the tight ringlet mirroring the anxiety twisting inside me.

"Thank you, Dr. Aberdeen," Tom interjected, sitting upright. "I've watched Doctors Inc grow from its inception, and I have plenty of ideas to improve our processes." His posture screamed confidence, as though he believed he was the obvious choice.

Dr. Aberdeen leaned back in his chair, a knowing smile curving his lips. "Let's not get ahead of ourselves, Tom. Everyone will have a chance to apply." It was clear then—Tom was never going to be the medical director.

"Well, I couldn't possibly accept the promotion," Karen said, feigning modesty. "Not with Brad's career rising so quickly." She gazed at her husband, cradling his chin like a prized trophy. "You know Brad's face is on a bus?"

My stomach churned. I set down my fork and took a long swig of my Old Fashioned, trying to wash away the bitterness. Karen wasn't fooling anyone. If she said she couldn't accept the promotion, it meant she fully intended to.

I couldn't let it happen. I couldn't let *Karen Chamberlain* become my boss. Even if it meant leaving myself no more chances to run from Ocean Hospital.

Pushing my doubt aside, I marched to the head of the table, a new speech forming in my mind. Letting go of my dream for a simple life, I placed a hand on Dr. Aberdeen's shoulder.

"Not now, Dr. Fahadi," he said dismissively. "I'm making an announcement. Take your seat."

"Dr. Aberdeen, this will only take a second," I insisted,

summoning every ounce of boldness I had. Tonight wasn't going to be my funeral. Tonight was going to be my rise.

"I want the promotion," I declared, my voice steady. I glanced at Isabelle whose satisfied smirk caused my own lips to curve up into a grin. "You know, I'm a real team player."

Six

By the time dinner and all its pivotal announcements were finished, nearly an hour had passed since I'd seen Tallahassee. The time had come to find him. His dreams had been crushed that day as well, and I couldn't shake the feeling that it was up to me to nurture, love, and repair what was unraveling between us. The Doctors Inc. group had mostly cleared out of the dining hall, leaving the staff to sweep up crumbs and flatware. But when I stepped into the ballroom, he wasn't at the bar. Instead, I found Opal back on her barstool, nursing a beer.

"Where's Tallahassee?" I asked, my voice betraying my urgency.

"He went to your room," she replied, patting the barstool next to her. The staff had dimmed the lights, and the atrium was emptying for the night.

"I can't stay. I need to find him."

"Isabelle wants to gather the Doctors Inc ladies in her hotel suite to try on gowns for the photoshoot," Opal announced.

"Really?" I frowned, my stomach tightening. With

Isabelle, there was always a price—and I had no doubt she'd make me pay it later.

"I'm not doing the photoshoot either," Opal added, oblivious to the mess of emotions tearing me in two directions—my new master's demands and my lover's unspoken needs. "I don't think baby weight and toddler puke stains are what *Le Crème* is going for."

"I can't go to Isabelle's room," I insisted, resolute. Showing Tallahassee that he mattered more than the shallow whims of Doctors Inc. felt vital—especially after they had so abruptly cut short our meeting with his parents just a week ago.

"Isabelle said you'd say that," Opal replied.

"Say what?"

"That you're not coming. I'm supposed to let Isabelle and Karen know."

"For God's sake, what more does she want from me?" I groaned, earning a sideways glance from the bartender. Shaking off the frustration, I firmed up my resolve and headed for the elevators. Before I could reach them, my handbag buzzed with a text. *It must be Tallahassee*, I thought with a flicker of nervous delight. But it wasn't.

Isabelle:

> Opal said you're not coming to my room? You should come! I want to treat the Doctors Inc ladies!

Another message followed almost immediately.

Karen:

> You should go to Isabelle's room. I would volunteer, but Brad is always buying clothes for me!

Of course, Karen would say that. I could practically see her in one of her obnoxious pantsuits, especially that burgundy one with matching heels. Who inspired her teased bangs—some 80s sitcom? Karen might be trying to convince me she didn't care about Isabelle's fashion advice, but I knew better—she could resist Isabelle's room about as well as her cats resisted tuna. No way was she passing up the chance to play her cards right. I rolled my eyes, tucked my phone away, and stepped into the elevator.

When I reached the tenth floor, Isabelle practically barreled into me, charging down the hall like a woman on a mission. "Nassrin! I brought some things for the photoshoot!" she exclaimed, her excitement bubbling over.

My pulse quickened as I gripped my room key like a lifeline, desperate to escape. "Not now, Isabelle," I said, turning to leave, but her footsteps echoed in time with mine. She was loaded down with a garment bag in one arm and an oversized Louis Vuitton bag in the other. "Let's talk in my room," she suggested with a smile that left no room for argument.

I sighed and took the heavy garment bag from her as we approached her door. "Did you pack all of Bealls department store in here?" I asked, attempting humor.

Isabelle laughed. "It's not Bealls. I had my stylist overnight some things from New York."

Right. Of course, Isabelle had a stylist. I may have been able to dodge Bealls winter dress line, but there was no way I was getting out of a curated collection from New York. I reluctantly shoved my room key back into my handbag as she unlocked her door. The room was a carbon copy of mine, but with a better view. Heaving the garment bag onto the couch, I unzipped it. A deep burgundy dress caught my eye. "Is this for Karen?"

"Karen is my backup plan," Isabelle said, checking her watch. "And she isn't here."

I smirked. "Karen told me Brad already completed her pantsuit wardrobe. She doesn't need your hand-me-downs."

Isabelle shook her head and laughed, her usual polished demeanor softening. "I'm obsessed with your look for this magazine!" she said, running a hand over the garments. Then she glanced at me with a mischievous glint in her eye. "Nassrin, I know you're hiding a boyfriend somewhere in this hotel. Why is he so important? Are you pregnant?"

I couldn't help but smile, despite myself. "No, but we're considering a dog."

"I had to drop out of medical school when Ronald and I got pregnant," Isabelle confided, and suddenly, I saw her in a new light. There was something raw and fascinating about her, a life lived boldly where I hesitated.

"You went to medical school?" I asked, genuinely curious.

"Ronald was my classmate," she said, smiling wistfully as she began draping gowns over chairs. "He lent me his pen after I chewed mine to bits... I didn't want to have an abortion, so... you know."

"Wow," I murmured, trailing my fingers over a sequined silver mini skirt. She was remarkable. She could have stayed in the medical grind and been just like me, but she chose to walk away—and somehow, that sacrifice only made her rise to something greater.

"What's his name—your boyfriend?" Isabelle asked, shifting focus.

"I call him Tallahassee," I replied, letting a playful grin slip through.

"Why?" she asked, glancing up from the jewelry she was arranging.

"So I don't get him confused with Gainesville," I quipped. But instead of laughing, Isabelle tensed, and my mind flashed to Tallahassee standing in The Pelican with his black eye and blue jeans. The doubts I always carried began to creep back in.

"Tallahassee must be running for Congress or something, the way you prioritize him," Isabelle said.

He wasn't running for Congress; he was a bartender. But he prioritized me, and that filled a missing piece of my heart. Still, I couldn't bring myself to correct her. Avoiding her gaze, I picked up a necklace and pretended to inspect it. "Yep. Tallahassee practically has his face on a bus."

"Listen, Nassrin. We're both from New York," Isabelle said, taking the necklace from me and pairing it with one of the gowns. "I'm Jewish. You're Palestinian. We celebrate the secular version of Christmas. It works. We know that diversity thrives up there. But in Gill-bert, Florida?" She shook her head. "Here, we have to work harder to show the world that Doctors Inc is diverse."

"Alex Tang can't wear pink?" I teased, holding up a brightly colored dress.

She laughed, a full, hearty sound. "It's not his color. Same for Tom!" She pulled a black gown from the bag and held it against my skin. "Doctors Inc needs to look like you. Go try this on."

I knew I was overdue to find Tallahassee—he'd come here for me, after all—but I relented, taking the gown to the bathroom. Isabelle and her beautiful gowns had won me over. The moment I slipped it on, I felt transformed. The gorgeous material shimmered in the mirror, making me feel invincible. Somewhere far off, a phone rang, but I ignored it. For a moment, I was untouchable.

When I returned to the room, my stomach dropped. Isabelle had my phone and was animatedly chatting. She wandered onto the balcony, clearly enjoying herself. When she spotted me, she smiled and waved me over.

"It's Tallahassee," she said, practically glowing. "I took the liberty of inviting him to the Christmas party." Then, in a whisper, she added, "Since you couldn't take my advice and leave him alone, I figured I'd better find out what's so special about him."

This was a disaster. I hadn't even mentioned the Christmas party to him yet, and here she was meddling. I lunged for the phone, my heart pounding. "Honey?" I said, breathless with apprehension.

"Babe, you didn't tell me about the photoshoot," his voice came through, rich with disappointment.

"It's complicated," I explained, stepping onto the balcony and sliding the door shut behind me. "But I can tell her no. It's only a photoshoot." I glanced back at Isabelle, satisfied she couldn't hear us.

"Are you sure?" he asked. "The lady made it sound important. Isn't she the one who overheard you badmouthing her husband?"

A gust of wind caught the gown's skirt, sending the fabric swirling around me. "Exactly. Isabelle overheard me rehearsing my resignation speech—the not-so-nice version. Your law school message didn't come in time. She's going to have me fired if I don't do what she wants."

"Oh, no." I heard him sigh through the phone. "Do you want me to beat her up?"

"Tallahassee!" I scolded but found that I was smiling. I squinted, darkness obscuring the waves below. I envisioned Karen Chamberlain becoming my boss, and the sight of her pantsuits haunted me.

"It is what it is," I replied, resignation heavy on my voice. I left the balcony and put an arm around Isabelle's bony shoulder.

"I'll bring you to the Christmas party with me," I told Tallahassee through the phone.

Isabelle squealed and grabbed the phone again. "I can't wait to meet you! It's formal attire. See you there!"

Seven

When I stowed the couture ball gown away and slipped back into my cocktail dress, my thoughts drifted to Tallahassee. The idea of finally returning to him filled me with relief. But, once again, my rival Karen was about to get in my way.

"I'm going to my room now," I told Isabelle, zipping up the garment bag with what little patience I had left.

"Karen should be here any minute," Isabelle said, tapping my hand gently. Her patronizing gesture was all it took to remind me of our roles—she held the cards, and I was expected to follow her lead. "Tea would be lovely, dear."

I clenched my teeth and rose to prepare the tea. My thoughts simmered over Karen. I had agreed to all of Isabelle's demands—why was I being forced to pretend that Karen was relevant? Karen was weak. Maybe I should brew the tea watered down and lukewarm, if that's what Isabelle liked.

A happy knock on the door interrupted my internal tirade, and when I opened it, Karen burst through, buzzing with energy. She hopped along on her high heels, her blond hair bouncing with every step.

"Isn't this exciting?" she asked, her eyes wide with uncontainable enthusiasm.

"*Le Crème,* yes, exciting," I replied flatly, shoving a Styrofoam cup into her hand before handing the other to Isabelle.

"Oh, I don't want *Le Crème,*" Karen said, waving me off with a dismissive flick of her wrist. "I've done so many photoshoots with my husband; I wouldn't feel right hogging the limelight."

"Your husband's face is on a bus, Karen," Isabelle said, her tone almost reverent. "You need *Le Crème* just to keep up." The adoration in her voice made me second guess her intentions. If she was bluffing, she had a great poker face.

"It's mine!" I blurted, flipping my hair defiantly over my shoulder. "Right, Isabelle?"

Isabelle feigned surprise, her eyebrows knitting together in an exaggerated display. "Oh, dear. I said we *want* you for the cover. I didn't say we *chose* you. Everyone in your division is being considered."

I searched her face for a hint of a wink, some shared secret that would confirm she was only teasing me. But Isabelle was too good at this. She didn't want me to feel special—she just wanted control. I felt my enthusiasm sink like stones in water, the wind leaving my sails.

"Nassrin, you need to work on your barista skills," Karen chortled, her laughter spilling over like soda pop. She gagged on the tea and dramatically dumped it down the sink as if it were poison.

Ignore it, I told myself. But as I watched Karen and Isabelle exchange a laugh, the words burned in my throat like acid. Isabelle took a languorous sip of her tea, a serene smile crossing her lips. She was playing us all, and she had the upper hand. If I was going to keep Karen from becoming the medical director, I would have to play, too. No one was going to hand it to me.

I held a bright pink dress up to Karen's frame. "None of these dresses seem quite right for you, Karen."

Karen snatched the dress and flung it on the bed. "I'm more concerned with my doctoring than I am with these gowns."

"How's your cat's feeding schedule going, anyway?"

"Someone should tell the other doctor to get up here," Isabelle interrupted, presumably referring to Opal. "I just want to make sure no one can claim they weren't included in the search for *Le Crème*."

"I mean, the only magazine that would put Opal Collins on the cover is *What Not to Wear*," Karen joked with a smirk. Their inauthenticity tightened like a knot around my gut. I wanted to take Opal and run.

"I don't think that's a magazine," Isabelle mused thoughtfully. "I think it was a television show from the nineties, but your point stands."

As if she could sense the betrayal hanging in the air, Opal arrived at that moment. Her ponytail was frazzled, stray hairs flying loose, and she had swapped her heels for sneakers—one of which had an untied shoelace flopping as she walked. She undid her scarf and handed it to me, the two wet spots on her dress still conspicuous. "You wanted to see me, Isabelle? What did I miss?" she asked, her smile bright and innocent.

"I just wanted to make sure you weren't trying to do the photoshoot. Or go for the medical director position. You aren't, are you, dear?" Isabelle asked, her gaze sweeping over Opal's attire with thinly veiled judgment.

Opal followed Isabelle's gaze down to her sneakers, her cheeks flushing. "I will one day, Isabelle. Not this time, but one day I will."

Isabelle clapped her hands, satisfied. "Okay. The article in *Le Crème* is going to print right after the New Year, ladies."

I wrung my hands, anxious for everyone to stop scrambling for Isabelle.

"Everything okay, Nassrin?" Opal asked, her cheeks still crimson from Isabelle's taunting.

"Everything is fine," I snapped.

It wasn't fine. I was ready to leave, ready to be with Tallahassee for the night. I was ready to be far from the women of Ocean Hospital.

"Are we done?" I asked.

"One more thing," Isabelle said, holding up a finger. "You girls can distribute this month's issue to the hospital wards. We want to increase readership before our article prints." She handed out stacks of *Le Crème,* oblivious to the storm brewing inside me. "Nassrin, should I count you in the running?"

I met her eyes, my resolve hardening. "Of course, Isabelle. Like you said, I'll be the face of Doctors Inc."

With that, I finally returned to Tallahassee. He was asleep in the bed, one arm thrown over my pillow. I crawled in next to him, savoring the warmth and calm he seemed to radiate. In the morning, I'd roll out from beneath his arm and plant a soft kiss on his forehead, treasuring the moment. He was everything I wasn't. He was the calm to my storm, the rest to my overwhelm.

But as I lay there, staring at the ceiling, the truth weighed on me—I was caught in a storm of my own making. Winning the photoshoot, outrunning Karen to the medical director position—those victories might keep me afloat while Tallahassee scrambled to steady himself. But they'd also consume me--consume the parts he needed most.

Eight

A week had passed since our night at The Pelican Hotel. Tallahassee had moved in with me temporarily, claiming that my presence helped him focus on filling out law school applications for his backup schools. While I spent long hours at Ocean Hospital, he lingered at home, shuffling through half-finished essays. In the evenings, I'd share stories about fascinating cases—only to watch his eyes glaze over when I tried to explain hyponatremia. I was straddling two worlds: one in the relentless pressure of healthcare, and another where he was still searching for a foothold.

In an instant, we were back at The Pelican, pulling into the grand entrance. In the last minutes before stepping out with Tallahassee for the world to see, I thought, *I can pull this off*. His black eye had nearly faded, leaving behind a faint yellow hue. I inspected the cufflinks on his rented tuxedo. He could pass for an ambitious politician or wealthy entrepreneur the way I had styled him. I had no intention of announcing that he was a failed law student with few prospects.

Tallahassee handed my keys to the valet. He flashed me that easy smile of his, and I took his arm, letting him lead me into the beachside ballroom. The holiday air crackled with excitement. I adjusted my black gown—tailored to perfection, with gold epaulets at the shoulders and fabric that sparkled like crystal ornaments on the Douglas firs scattered around the hotel. Isabelle had insisted it was couture, straight from a New York design house, and I had to admit, it accentuated my curves beautifully.

Tallahassee had insisted on paying for the tuxedo rental, surprising me by upgrading to the best package from Men's Wearhouse. As we walked into the ballroom, I glanced around, subtly comparing his tux to the sea of black coats. He blended in perfectly. Unlike the chaos of women's attire—magnificent ball gowns here, frumpy slacks and sneakers there—the men's suits were uniform, near-identical. The only distinctions were the occasional bulky pagers clipped to doctors' belts and tumblers filled with soda instead of scotch. Tallahassee circled his arm around my waist, and I reassured myself that all was well.

A crowd was gathering for the photoshoot. Dr. Aberdeen was about to announce his choice for medical director, and the shoot would follow. Tom stood by a column, sipping a martini in a green three-piece suit that popped against his brown skin. He looked smug, like he already knew he'd won. Opal was there, arm linked with her husband, and even Alex had made an effort with a bow tie and baggy slacks. Karen, of course, was impossible to miss. Her crimson gown screamed Christmas cheer, and she'd teased her bangs to twice their natural height. I half expected her to show up in that burgundy pantsuit, but Karen would never make that mistake.

I wove through the raucous partygoers and perched on a barstool, leaning into the crowd to eavesdrop as Isabelle gave instructions to a magazine reporter and photographer. Her eyes flicked toward me as she gestured in my direction. *It's happening,* I thought.

The set for the shoot was breathtaking. The Pelican's soaring columns rose twenty feet before curving into magnificent arches. Checkerboard tile, original to the hotel, flowed seamlessly from the ballroom to the terrace, framing a moody ocean and a clear sky. Soon, the sun would paint ripples of orange, red, and pink across the horizon. It was the perfect backdrop.

The photographer approached me—a man with dark hair and a rebellious leather jacket that stood out against the formal crowd. "Are you the one we're shooting?" he asked.

"That's what I hear," I replied, trying to sound nonchalant.

He smiled. "That's great. Come over and take some test shots. We're going for a natural look, you know? Think 'highbrow artsy.'"

I nodded toward Dr. Aberdeen. "We probably have to wait for him to make it official."

The photographer chuckled. "Right. Got it. I just assumed his wife was in charge. In that case, I'm on a smoke break." He disappeared out the back, leaving me alone with my thoughts.

Dr. Aberdeen eventually made his way over to us, gripping Tallahassee's hand in a firm shake. "I've heard a lot about you, son," he said, beaming.

My stomach tightened. If that were true, there was no way he would approve. What could he have heard? *Tallahassee is a bartender in a college town, serving drinks to intoxicated students. He specializes in Spring Break.*

"Likewise," Tallahassee replied smoothly, matching Ronald's strength in the handshake. His hand went straight from Dr. Aberdeen's back to mine.

Isabelle appeared, lighting up when she saw Tallahassee. "So, this is who you've been keeping from us!" she exclaimed looking him up and down.

I wanted to stay by his side, but Isabelle had other plans. She took me by the elbow, pulling my hand from Tallahassee's and leading me away. Dressed in gold fabric with a plunging neckline, she had added an airbrushed tan and a gold pelican pendant that cleverly concealed the wrinkles along her neck.

"You'll sit on that tree stump, and I'll be behind you with my hand on your shoulder," Isabelle explained, pointing to the props on the set.

I glanced back at Tallahassee, still stuck in conversation with Dr. Aberdeen, and answered absently, "I thought we were doing highbrow artsy."

"Please, dear," Isabelle said with a dismissive wave. "I'm not leaving anything to chance on the cover of *Le Crème*." She paused, studying me. "I see you can't wait to get back to him. Go."

I didn't need to be told twice. I rushed back to Tallahassee, finding him exactly where I'd left him, enduring one of Dr. Aberdeen's stories about gastrointestinal research. He caught my eye and gave me a subtle nod that clearly said, *save me*.

"Let's go see Opal," I suggested, taking his arm and leading him into the crowd.

"Nassrin!" Opal exclaimed when we approached. "Have I mentioned that your boyfriend is gorgeous?" Her gaze lingered on Tallahassee, admiration plain on her face. "How could you let such a pretty face get into a boxing ring?"

I sighed. "Okay, Pretty Face. Maybe you could go to the bar and get some drinks so I can talk about you behind your back," I teased, winking at him. He grinned and headed off.

"A boxer?" Tom asked, his eyebrows arching in interest. "I didn't realize you were dating a martial artist. You know, I did some street fighting back in the day." His wife chuckled, giving him an affectionate smack on the arm.

"What does he do?" Opal's husband asked.

"Well..." I began, but Karen barged in, dragging Brad

along with her, both bubbling with holiday cheer. Brad, juggling a tray of cocktails, whooped as he handed out drinks.

"Are we talking about Nassrin's boy toy?" Karen asked, narrowing her eyes suspiciously at Tallahassee, who was chatting animatedly with the bartender across the room. "Nassrin, tell us what he does!"

"Well, as you know, he lives in Tallahassee," I said, my heart racing. Dr. Aberdeen and Isabelle had joined the group, their presence sending my confidence into a nosedive. It was if his struggle to succeed would cast a shadow on me, as though his failures were my own. The thought of my accomplished colleagues discovering the truth--he didn't come close to their success--filled me with dread. I couldn't stand the idea of their unveiled judgment, comparisons that would leave me feeling exposed and ashamed.

"Now there's a man's man!" Dr. Aberdeen said, his eyes gleaming as he pointed toward Tallahassee. "He looks like a guy we could use at Doctors Inc. I could tell by his handshake!"

I gulped, watching Tallahassee stride toward us with drinks in hand, his confidence unshaken. I took a step back, panic surging.

"What department can I put him in, Nassrin? Is he a doctor? Accounting? Should I put him on the Board of Directors?" Dr. Aberdeen's eyes sparkled with genuine enthusiasm.

Karen cackled, and I felt the anxiety rise to a breaking point. "He's a lawyer!" I blurted, the words escaping before I could stop them. My voice sounded more certain than I felt.

"Well, we can put him in legal, then," Dr. Aberdeen said, his grin widening.

Tallahassee reached me just as I began to spiral. I pulled him into a kiss, desperate to keep him from saying anything that might unravel my lie. If Dr. Aberdeen realized that I lied to his face to save my own skin, I wouldn't be getting a promotion now or ever.

"There you are, honey," I said, my voice soft but urgent. "Let's get some air."

He agreed, and we slipped away toward the terrace. But as we stepped outside, I heard footsteps behind us. Turning, I saw Dr. Aberdeen trotting after us.

"Nassrin," he called, his face alight with excitement. "Imagine *Le Crème* featuring you two as a power couple. Son, are you up for a photoshoot tonight?"

Nine

I glanced toward the bar, where Tallahassee had wandered after Dr. Aberdeen's invitation to be in the photoshoot. Comfortably immersed in conversation with the bartender, his laughter rang out, light and carefree, like Christmas bells. I could hear him marveling over Doctors Inc and their acceptance of him, as if *Le Crème* had opened its glossy arms to embrace him. "Can you believe it?" he said, his voice carrying through the room. "A bartender, featured in a magazine, with a beautiful woman at his side?"

I cringed. *Stop talking*, I begged silently. The minutes dragged on, refusing to end as we all waited for Dr. Aberdeen to reveal his choice for medical director. The partygoers held their breath, anticipation heavy in the air. I tried to disappear, wringing my hands as Isabelle barked instructions to the photographer to adjust the layout—now accounting for Tallahassee. Her eyes flicked toward me.

"Nassrin, you're getting frown lines," she chided, her tone sharp as ever. "Come stand in front of the Christmas tree so the photographer can take a few test shots."

"Just let me grab Tallahassee first," I said quickly, my voice tight. Without waiting for her response, I dashed toward the bar. Could I get him to keep quiet and still maintain the façade?

But before I could reach him, Brad Lessons sidled up to the photographer, Karen clinging to his arm like an accessory. "It's now or never," Brad said to his wife before slipping into a barstool right next to Tallahassee.

I froze, caught awkwardly between the bar and the set—between my lover and my career. My unease mounted as I stood there, torn.

"Isabelle," Karen said, grasping Isabelle's elbow with a practiced air of entitlement. "You need to talk to Ronald about making me medical director."

"Not now, dear," she replied, pulling her elbow free. "I think he's going in another direction."

Karen squinted at me, and for a moment, I wanted to give up—pack up my bartender boyfriend and disappear. But there was nowhere to go. If Karen became the medical director, she'd turn the department into her personal kingdom, delegating every ounce of work to the rest of us while she reaped the rewards. Barking orders through smudged lipstick, she'd drain us, all while cementing her untouchable position. I couldn't let that happen—I couldn't give up yet.

Laughter erupted from the bar behind me, pulling my attention back to Tallahassee. "A Rusty Pelican includes whiskey and orange bitters," the bartender explained, mixing drinks with a practiced ease.

"A Rusty Pelican should have rum and grenadine!" Tallahassee sang back, his voice full of lighthearted confidence. The men laughed together like old friends.

I took a step back, panic rising. Should I stop Karen or Tallahassee? If he found out I lied about him being a lawyer—then what? The thought made me sick. I didn't want to find out.

"Well, let's have one of each," Brad suggested, his voice carrying back toward me. "A Rusty Pelican from the bartender and a Rusty Pelican from the big-shot lawyer."

My heart dropped. I pounced toward the bar, but it was too late. The damage was done. My lie was exposed, and Karen had already claimed my place in front of the camera, a smug grin plastered across her face.

Tallahassee's expression crumpled, his easy confidence shattering into confusion. He got to his feet just as I reached him, my couture gown trailing behind me like a river of betrayal.

"Why did Brad just call me a big-shot lawyer?" he asked, his tone raw with hurt and bewilderment.

"Don't take it seriously," I said quickly, panting as I clung to his arm. "He's just being dramatic."

He shook me off, and the look on his face cut deeper than his old black eye ever had. "So, you didn't want your friends to find out I was just a bartender?"

Across the room, Isabelle dismissed the photographer with a wave of her hand. "Take another smoke break," she said absently, her attention fixed on my commotion. I wanted to crawl into a hole, to disappear entirely, but Isabelle was already sauntering over. She sized up Tallahassee with a scrutinizing gaze, grabbing the collar of his jacket and peering at the label.

"Men's Wearhouse," she scoffed. "I thought it looked cheap."

"Isabelle!" I cried, my voice cracking with a mix of anger and desperation. Before I could say more, Karen paraded over, patting her hair sprayed bangs back into place.

"What are we talking about? What did I miss?" she asked with a smirk.

"I'm just a bartender," Tallahassee said flatly, the words hitting me like a blow.

"Don't go!" I pleaded, my voice breaking. I couldn't let him leave.

The bartender slid two Rusty Pelicans across the bar—tall tumblers brimming with brightly colored liquid. Tallahassee picked one up, swirling the contents before taking a sip. "See? Grenadine," he said, setting the glass down with a thud. And then he was gone, pushing through the crowd toward the terrace.

"We may need to rethink this photoshoot," Karen said, appearing at Brad's side and giving him a wink. "Nassrin's dress will fit me if we pin it at the waist."

Summoning the restraint to keep myself from punching her in the mouth, I looked past her, searching for Tallahassee. He was gone. Instead, I found Dr. Aberdeen rushing to the bar. He stopped at Isabelle's side.

"What did you do to Nassrin's boyfriend?" he demanded of Isabelle. "He was supposed to do the photoshoot."

"He's not a lawyer," Isabelle answered with an exaggerated roll of her eyes. "Apparently, he's just a bartender. Nassrin can do it without him."

"Brad is a real lawyer," Karen chimed in smugly. "He's on a bus. Let's get on with this. Can you please tell the others that I'm going to be the medical director?"

I stood there, frozen, as they picked apart my life like buzzards. But I couldn't let it end this way. I wouldn't. "I'm not letting you take the photoshoot," I said firmly, setting my jaw. But even as I spoke, my heart screamed at me to run, to chase Tallahassee and fix the mess I had created.

Ronald towered over me, and I shrunk into the barstool. "Nassrin, the man I saw run to the terrace is devastated. He may not be a big shot like we are, but he's got something special. If you don't go out there and fix it, he'll be gone. I'll let you decide, Dr. Fahadi."

Isabelle stepped in front of him, wagging a bony finger at

me. "If you don't get on that set and do the photoshoot right now, I swear I will tell Ronald everything you said about him!"

My eyes darted between the two Aberdeens. Ronald smirked. "What'd you say about me?"

I'm tired of your stupid hospital! Your leadership is terrible, and I quit. The memory of my own words came back to haunt me.

Without another thought, I kicked off my shoes and bolted through the crowded ballroom.

"Nassrin, the dress!" Karen called after me, but I didn't look back. I kept running, weaving through the crowd until I burst onto the terrace overlooking the sea.

Ten

The sun dipped low, casting a kaleidoscope of colors across the sky above The Pelican. Mellow oranges and reds blended together, chased by soft pinks and purples reflecting from the clouds, heralding the night's arrival. I dropped the hem of my gown and clung to the terrace railing, forcing myself to breathe. Behind me, I could hear the photographer scrambling to capture the next face of Doctors Inc. The relentless click of his camera punctuated my racing thoughts.

Tallahassee stood at the edge of the terrace, his gaze fixed on the horizon. He wouldn't even look at me.

"I'm sorry," I whispered, my voice barely audible over the distant waves. He didn't respond. His rented jacket lay draped over a café chair, abandoned. The top button of his shirt was undone, and my eyes traced the strong line of his jaw to his collarbone. He was perfect—how had I missed it in the chaos of our turmoil? "I'm sorry," I said again, this time with resignation slipping into my words.

"You're ashamed of me," he said finally, his voice heavy. The weight of storm clouds gathering in the west pressed down on us.

"No," I insisted, shaking my head.

"Don't deny it, Nassrin. I embarrass you." He wrestled with one of his cufflinks, frustration flashing across his face as he yanked it free. Wisps of black clouds drifted in front of the sun, fracturing its light.

"These people are different," I murmured, my chest aching as the words left my mouth. "I wanted to protect you." But even as I said it, I felt the lie lodge in my throat. My lies were never about protecting him.

Tallahassee spun around to face me, his expression raw and pained. "You wanted to protect yourself!" he cried. "I thought it was cute when you called me Tallahassee. But now I see—it was just a way to keep me separate from your real life!"

"Why didn't you just tell them about law school?" I shot back, desperation creeping into my voice. "Why not explain that soon it'll be your face on the bus?"

"Because I don't need their approval!" he shouted. "I'm fine with who I am." His words hit me like a slap, and as twilight turned to night, the tension between us unraveled like a fraying thread. A low rumble of thunder echoed in the distance. The flashing lights from the photographer's camera could have been lightning igniting our storm.

Why had I fought so hard for their approval? It was as if I needed their approval for validation. I didn't need any of that now. I just needed Tallahassee, plain and simple. I never had to choose between him and medicine; I already had it all.

"I'm glad you brought me here, Nassrin," he said, his voice quieter now but no less firm. "Better to find out now—better to learn how willing you are to sacrifice me for their approval. You can have them. I'm done."

"I'm not done, Tallahassee. This doesn't feel like the end," I said, my voice trembling but resolute. I reached around my back, fumbling for the eye hook holding my dress in place. "I would give up all of this for you."

"What are you doing?" he gasped as raindrops began to fall, one stinging my cheek like a tear. The hook released, and the gown slumped from my shoulders.

"I don't need couture ball gowns or *Le Crème,*" I declared. "I need you." Without him, I could diagnose a thousand broken hearts, but I couldn't begin to mend my own.

Shrugging off the dress, I let it pool at my feet. Only my slip remained, fragile and revealing. Vulnerability replaced my defenses, and I hoped it would bridge the chasm between us.

"Tallahassee," I murmured, teasing him with a sway of my hips. I felt the murmurs ripple through the scattered party-goers behind me, their eyes fixed on me as whispers spilled into the ballroom. I stepped onto the staircase that led down to the sand, letting the cool grains greet my toes with each step. The crashing waves called me forward, grounding me in the moment. I would do whatever it took to remind him of our first date, back when everything felt simple and right. It had started at a beach not unlike this one.

I glanced back toward The Pelican, glowing warmly from within. No one rushed to stop me. There was only Tallahassee, his white shirt glowing like a beacon in the dark. My heart ached to cling to him again.

But I turned back to the sea, pressing forward. The water swirled around my ankles, then my knees, until I dove beneath the surface. Cool waves embraced me, washing away the makeup that had made me picture-perfect. As I broke through the surface, I felt something new—liberation. My feet sank into the sandy bottom as I turned back to the shore.

But before I could find him, a powerful wave crashed into me, tumbling me forward.

I wasn't afraid. I'd spent countless summers in the ocean; I knew how to handle its unpredictable pull. But this felt different. I regained my footing, the saltwater stinging my eyes as I imagined Tallahassee forgiving me. I pictured how we could rebuild, this time on a foundation of honesty. Even if he couldn't let go of the past, I was ready to prove I could be better for our future. Losing him had made one thing clear—I was ready to make *us* my priority.

Another wave barreled into me, more forceful than the last, dragging me under. The water tugged at my hair and limbs, rolling me like a leaf caught in a storm. Panic bubbled beneath the surface, but I fought it back as I resurfaced, sputtering and gasping for air. I wiped tangled strands of hair from my face, treading water as fear crept into my chest.

The tide had pulled me out. The shore was shrinking, slipping farther and farther away as the current carried me to sea.

"Tallahassee!" I screamed, desperation tearing through my voice. But the figure that had glowed like a ray of hope only moments ago was gone, swallowed by the night.

Eleven

Two Years Earlier

The 8-year-old Dodge Neon had definitely seen better days. Tallahassee was its third owner, but I couldn't help noticing the little things he'd done to it—replacing the windshield wipers, fixing the paint job, tinkering with the spark plugs. In the short time he'd had it, he'd added his own touches to keep it running. I didn't suggest taking my BMW to Honeymoon Island because I didn't want to add any unnecessary miles. Instead, we cleared out the remnants of fast food—hamburger wrappers and a few wayward French fries—to make room for our beach bag.

The bag was stuffed to the brim with everything we could possibly need: towels, sunscreen, a straw hat for me, a ball cap for him, magazines, the book I'd started last summer, a laptop, water, snacks, and even a bottle of wine. Tallahassee tossed it onto the back seat without much care, where it landed on a foundation of sand left over from some prior adventure.

As we cruised down the interstate, the radio hummed with the infectious beat of Ace of Base. The music blended perfectly with the feeling of escape—carefree and vibrant. I smoothed out the wrinkles in my new swim cover, a thrill of adventure bubbling in my chest. This was our first long drive together, and it felt like a precious moment, so different from my day-to-day grind: fluorescent lights, a relentless pace, and the constant pressure weighing on me. It had been my idea to take this strange new man from Tallahassee all the way to Honeymoon Island.

"So, what's at Honeymoon Island?" he asked, switching the music from Ace of Base to Kenny Chesney's *Summertime.*

I smiled, glancing over at him. "It's a state park—so, really just an ice cream stand, but that's part of the charm." My mind flickered back to the night before, when I'd first met him. Two single girlfriends unwinding in the capital city, and I'd somehow found myself enchanted by the bartender mixing drinks and sneaking me free pours. He was charging everyone else, but not me. It was such a cliché, and I was such a fool—but somehow, here we were.

"I like you already," he said, flashing me a radiant smile that sent butterflies fluttering in my stomach.

The clock ticked toward 10:00 AM as the miles melted away. Hours of being awake had made my eyelids heavy, and I felt myself drifting closer to sleep when a wave of warm, humid air jolted me awake. I turned to see Tallahassee rolling down his window.

"The AC went out," he said with an apologetic shrug.

I yawned and rolled my own window down. "Should we stop for freon?" he asked.

I laughed lightly. "I don't even know what freon is. But it's not much farther, right?"

The sun poured down on us with relentless heat at every red light, baking us alive. Just when I thought I couldn't take it anymore, raindrops began to splatter against my arm. I looked over to see Tallahassee frowning at the sky. "It wasn't supposed to rain today," he said. "Should we stop?"

"I mean, we were planning to get wet at the beach

anyway," I reasoned, though doubt was creeping in. Had we wasted the day, driving for hours only to get caught in the rain? The sky opened up, and soon the rain was pouring in through the open windows, soaking our laps.

"We have to put the windows up!" he exclaimed. I cranked mine closed, already mourning the last bit of ventilation. "Should we turn around?" he asked.

"Just a little farther," I insisted, trying to push back my growing anxiety. By the time we reached the Dunedin Causeway, the rain and lack of AC had fogged up the windshield so badly that we could barely see. Tallahassee slowed the car to a crawl as I grabbed a towel from the bag, wiping at the glass. But for every patch I cleared, new fog rushed in to mock me.

"We can turn around," I whispered, barely audible over the pounding rain.

"Hey, I can hang if you can," he replied with that easy smile of his. He lowered his window farther and leaned out like a carefree dog, letting the rain pelt his face as thunder rumbled overhead.

At long last, we pulled up to the tiny shack marking the entrance to the park. The parking lot was empty, the ranger's booth unmanned. Tallahassee grabbed a towel and draped it over my shoulders as we stepped out into the rain. I picked my way through the rocky terrain, cheeks burning with embarrassment. This wasn't how I'd pictured our day. We didn't know each other well enough for this to feel funny yet—it just felt like a disaster. The park was desolate, the solitude amplifying my foolishness.

"Come on," Tallahassee said, taking my hand. He led me toward the waves, his grip steady and warm. "We'll feel warmer in the water." Relief coursed through me as I squeezed his hand, and together, we dashed into the surf.

When the water reached our necks, he wrapped his arms around me, pulling me close. "We have to watch for rip currents," he murmured. "They're likely to form after a storm."

I nodded, pressing against his chest and feeling the rhythm of his heartbeat sync with mine. The rain mingled with the ocean around us, and when he lifted my chin, our lips met in a kiss that sent electricity coursing through every nerve in my body. It was perfection. When I opened my eyes, sunlight was breaking through the clouds, casting a shimmering rainbow across the sky—a beautiful reward for our commitment to this stolen day on Honeymoon Island.

"Cue the dolphin," Tallahassee said with a grin, pointing toward the waves where a pod of dolphins rolled playfully in the surf.

"This is perfect," I breathed, my heart soaring as I kissed him again. In that moment, I realized he was my anchor to stability.

TWELVE
PRESENT DAY

"NASSRIN!" TALLAHASSEE'S VOICE BOOMED OVER the crashing waves as he sprinted down the staircase toward the raging surf. "It's a rip current! Swim parallel to the shore!" His arm pointed forcefully to the north, urgency burning in his eyes. How could I have been so careless? The storm brewing around us had been a warning, and I ignored it. Turning my body, I paddled with everything I had, pushing against the water's relentless pull.

Then I saw him throw himself into the turbulence without hesitation—shirt, pants, and shoes still on. My heart clenched as I watched him swim toward me, his strong, steady strokes cutting through the roaring waves. I gasped as another wave submerged me, saltwater searing my throat as I struggled to keep my head above water. He was getting closer, but not fast enough.

After an eternity, I finally broke free from the current's grip. My arms and legs burned, my chest heaved, and I leaned back, desperate to keep floating. Just as exhaustion threatened to drag me under again, I felt Tallahassee's arm wrap firmly around my chest.

I opened my eyes to see him beside me, his hair plastered to his forehead, his breath coming in ragged bursts as he pulled us both toward the shore. His strength was my lifeline, and I clung to it with everything I had.

"I'm sorry," I murmured, my voice barely audible over the crashing waves. But when his eyes flicked toward mine, I couldn't help but smile. "This reminds me of Honeymoon Island."

He let out a breathless laugh, a playful glint breaking through the worry in his eyes. "This is nothing like Honeymoon Island," he teased as his feet found the ground and he planted me firmly on solid sand. "Except for the beach, the storm, and the unlikely swim in the Gulf."

An attendant from The Pelican rushed toward us with a blanket, scolding me for my recklessness. But Tallahassee waved him off, wrapping the blanket around my shoulders with a protective tenderness. He guided me to a café chair on the terrace, his presence a warm shelter from the storm raging both above us and within me.

"Now," he said, crouching in front of me, his brows knitting together. "What were you thinking?"

I stared past him, my eyes fixed on the waves crashing rhythmically on the shore. "I guess I thought if I could replicate Honeymoon Island, I could fix this."

His expression softened, but the weight of his words hit me hard. "I don't belong here," he said, his voice calm but resolute. "But you do."

My gaze dropped to the sand clinging to his soaked shoes and the way his shirt clung to his chest. "You're right," I whispered, avoiding his eyes. "I could have had you and kept being a doctor." I swiped at the tears that were gathering in my eyes. "A really good doctor, too. But it might be too late for me."

"If you say so," he said simply, turning to look out at the horizon as thunder rumbled ominously in the distance.

Was it too late? Could I really lose everything—Doctors Inc and Tallahassee—in one night? The irony twisted in my chest like a knife. I had wanted nothing more than a simple life, and yet here I was, saved by my knight in soaked armor, emptier than ever.

It had taken nearly drowning to see it. My life didn't belong in anyone's hands but my own. I should seize control and write my own story. If the Aberdeens didn't fire me, I would stay at Ocean Hospital, not for money or magazine covers, but for the satisfaction of doing good in the world.

A surge of determination coursed through me, as strong and unstoppable as the rip current. "I'm going inside," I said suddenly, rising to my feet. "I'll stand side by side with you as an equal, if you'll let me. If you aren't here when I get back, I'll understand. But I hope you are." I squeezed his shoulders then draped the blanket over them. Then I turned and dashed toward the back entrance of The Pelican, my heart racing with fear, resolve, and something new—hope.

The back hallway felt surreal, bustling with staff and valet workers who stared openly at my soaked slip and tangled hair. I ignored them, my focus fixed forward, until I crashed directly into Isabelle.

She grabbed my shoulders, shaking me as if I'd lost my mind. "What has gotten into you?" she demanded.

"You should be ashamed of the way you treated Tallahassee!" I snapped, my anger flaring before I could stop myself. The words tumbled out, sharp and unrelenting.

"Probably, dear," she replied breezily, as if I'd accused her of stealing cookies from a jar. "But I honestly can't remember what I did." She motioned for me to follow. "We need to talk."

I caught a glimpse of the ballroom as a waiter pushed through a nearby door. Dr. Aberdeen stood in the center of a lively conversation with Karen and Brad, laughter ringing out, now unable to injure my pride. The door swung shut again, and I turned back to Isabelle.

"Karen isn't the right fit for medical director," Isabelle said, her tone friendly.

"Why not?" I asked with nonchalance.

"Because she's lazy, and she'll cause Ronald a headache for the next decade if we don't act now."

The absurdity of it all hit me, and for a moment, I laughed —a short, bitter exhale. Isabelle wanted to live out her own dreams through me. She remained unflinching, however.

"It has to be you, Nassrin," she continued. "Even with your... issues regarding that bartender."

The way she said *bartender*—like it was the flu—made my chest ache. I knew the truth. Isabelle Aberdeen would never accept me while I was tied to Tallahassee.

"I don't want it anymore," I said quietly. "Tell Dr. Aberdeen everything. Let him fire me. I choose love."

I broke free from her grasp. "I'm sorry, Isabelle. Karen is your woman now." And with that, I left her standing there and found what I was looking for—a hotel phone in a quiet corner.

"Mrs. Newsome?" I said when his mother answered. My voice trembled as I poured my heart out, apologizing for letting my insecurities threaten my relationship with her son. I begged for her support, though I didn't need to. Her kindness was immediate, her voice gentle as she gave her blessing.

"Go talk to him," she urged. "Tell him his mother gives her blessing."

"Thank you," I whispered, gripping the receiver before carefully placing it back in the cradle.

As I tiptoed back to the terrace, I found Dr. Aberdeen blocking my path. His eyes were stern, and his arms were folded. "Isabelle says you hate me and my stupid company," he said.

I adopted his posture and folded my arms, screwing up my face to match his. "Fire me if you want."

He sighed. "I'm not going to fire you, Nassrin. You're the best doctor we've got. But I am giving the promotion to Karen."

He scanned my damp ensemble from head to toe. "I hope you understand."

I leapt at him, throwing my arms around his expensive suit. "Thank you!" I cried.

He peeled me off and held me at arm's length. "Go on," he urged. "Go find your better half."

My heart pounded as I returned to the terrace. The sconces lining the path cast a soft glow on the tiles, each step bringing me closer to him. But when I reached the place where he had been, Tallahassee was gone.

My heart sank. I searched the dark, the rain still dancing to its own rhythm. The blanket was folded neatly on the table, and someone had placed my shoes beside the chair.

I sighed, sinking into the chair and wriggling out of his jacket. I'd have to return it to Men's Wearhouse. Being wrapped in the chill of my own mistakes felt more fitting now. As I buckled the strap of my high heel, the night's strangeness settled over me. I had arrived determined to be the face of Doctors Inc. Now I was about to leave single, and with seaweed in my hair.

A tap on my shoulder made me jump. I turned to see Tallahassee standing there, framed in the soft light of the sconce, a sandy bouquet of daisies and clovers in his hand.

“Nassrin,” he said, his voice low and steady, thick with emotion. “I want to be here. I just need to know you want me too.” He held out the scruffy bouquet.

“I called your mom,” I whispered, taking the flowers and burying my face against his chest. “I told her everything. She gave us her blessing.”

He smiled, wrapping his arms around me. For a moment, we stood there—two people anchored to one another in a world full of expectations.

"I'll finish law school, Nassrin. And then you can leave Doctors Inc—or stay. You can be whoever you want to be."

"Right now," I said, my voice soft but sure, "I just want to be with you."

"I'm going to start calling you Gill-bert," he teased.

I laughed as I kissed him, saltwater dripping from our clothes. The seaweed in my hair had dried into a salty crust.

A burst of light startled me, and I turned to see the photographer capturing the moment. His leather jacket disappeared into the night as the camera clicked away.

"This is exactly what *Le Crème* is looking for," the photographer said, taking one last shot.

Thirteen

The photoshoot had ended, the moment captured and passed. While the rest of The Pelican celebrated, I slid into a terrace chair, pulling Tallahassee down beside me. The night air was cool against my damp skin, and the chaos inside felt like a distant memory.

Opal emerged onto the terrace, mercifully leaving the others behind. She took a seat at our table, resting a reassuring hand on my shoulder.

"It's alright, Nassrin," she said gently, her voice warm. "This probably happens all the time." Her eyes flicked to my drenched hair and the $3,000 gown crumpled in a heap at my feet. She couldn't hold back a laugh, and honestly, neither could I. What was next for me? I had no idea.

"Seriously," Opal urged, her tone softening but insistent. "We need you back inside."

"Sorry, Opal. This night is over for me." I glanced at Tallahassee, then back to her. "So, Karen's our new medical director?"

"Yes," Opal replied, a hint of mischief in her voice, "but

don't worry. She'll be on the cover of *Le Crème* with lipstick on her teeth."

Opal patted my hand, then turned her attention to Tallahassee, her smile widening. "If we can't have Nassrin back inside, can we at least have you?"

He raised an eyebrow. "Me?"

"Something about a Rusty Pelican," Opal teased. "Dr. Aberdeen liked your drink so much he ordered a round of Rusty Pelicans for everyone at the party." She gestured toward the ballroom, where a growing line snaked from the bar, waitstaff scrambling to keep up with orders.

"Opal, can you give us a minute?" I asked, needing space to sort through the whirlwind of emotions swirling inside me.

"Sure," she said with a knowing wink, gliding away. "The party needs Tallahassee STAT. My husband's trying to help the bartender, but he keeps going too heavy on the rum!" She draped my dress over the back of the chair and left us alone.

I turned to Tallahassee, my voice soft but steady. "I got so carried away with the photoshoot, I never stopped to take care of you." I studied his face, feeling the weight of the night slowly lifting. "I've spent so much time dreaming of making a simple life with you, I didn't recognize I already had it."

His expression softened, love shining in his eyes. "Nassrin, I loved you for you. You never had to be someone else."

"It isn't your law degree that's going to give me a simple life. And it's not being a doctor that's going to keep me from it. I have everything I need right now because I have you. The rest will come," I said excitedly.

"The rest will come," he echoed, his voice filled with certainty.

I stood from the table, letting the blanket fall to the ground. Picking up my gown, I inspected it—it was soaked with seawater. I stepped into it and turned to him, my heart racing as his hands brushed against my skin, firm and reassuring as he zipped up the back.

As the clasp clicked into place, I finally exhaled. We had walked through fire and come out burned, but alive. He kissed me then, with a passion that ignited the world around us, and a tear slid down my cheek. In that moment, I felt it—the flame between us was still burning strong.

"Can you show me how to mix a Rusty Pelican?" I asked, breathless and playful.

"No," he said firmly, though the teasing smile on his face softened the refusal. He took my hand, guiding me toward the bar. "You know how it took eight years of school to be a doctor?" he asked, slipping behind the counter.

"I think I know where this is going," I replied, grinning.

"Oh, thank God," Opal's husband exclaimed as we approached. He slid a bottle of rum toward Tallahassee before retreating, leaving us with the tools of his trade.

I grabbed the bottle, ready to dive into his world.

"Not so fast, pretty lady," Tallahassee said with a beam. "You have to pass the dishwasher exam before you can tend the bar." He pointed toward the sink, stacked high with tumblers, their abandoned contents a testament to the night.

I laughed, the sound bright and freeing, cutting through the din of the party. Never had I been so grateful to wash a glass. We had started this romance on opposite sides of the bar, and now here we were standing side by side. And although I wasn't doing any of it well, we were together and my messy life was complete.

Cheers erupted as Tallahassee poured the first round of drinks, sliding them across the counter with a flourish. We laughed and shared stories, the night transforming into something celebratory.

Then Opal approached with a microphone in hand. She flicked the switch, and the crowd hushed, their curiosity piqued. "Friends of Doctors Inc," she began, her voice commanding the room's attention. "I'd like to make a toast."

From the corner of my eye, I saw Isabelle and Karen push their way to the front like hungry cats called to supper. "To a new era!" Opal declared.

"Cheers!" the crowd roared back.

Opal locked eyes with the photographer from *Le Crème*. "I've been told *Le Crème* has stumbled across a most amazing cover shot for the magazine." She gestured toward us, the disheveled couple, and the photographer bowed dramatically. The crowd cheered again. "Something highbrow and artsy!" Opal added with a grin.

Isabelle made a move for the microphone, but Opal skillfully thwarted her, handing it to me instead. My heart skipped a beat as I climbed onto the bar, Tallahassee steadying me with a hand on my arm. A leftover shred of kelp clung to my shoulder, and I tapped the microphone, finding my voice amid the cheers.

"And cheers to Tallahassee," I said, my voice ringing out. "Without whom there would be no Rusty Pelicans!"

"Cheers!" The crowd echoed back with booming enthusiasm.

Tallahassee pulled me into his arms, and as the storm within me finally settled, I realized something profound. I wasn't going to be the medical director, but I wasn't going to resign either. With Tallahassee by my side, I felt stronger than ever—stronger than Doctors Inc, stronger than the expectations weighing on me. I was ready to face whatever came next.

"And without whom I would be lost," I added, raising my glass.

The crowd cheered again, their energy electrifying the air. For the first time in a long time, I felt whole.

The End

What's next? Visit jaceybici.kit.com to find out.

That Kind of Girl

We hope you enjoyed The Pelican Hotel by Jacey Bici. If you'd like to hear more about Ocean Hospital or you're dying to know Tallahassee's real name, be sure to read That Kind of Girl, a novel by Jacey Bici.

For links to your favorite retailer for print, ebook, and audiobook, visit https://books.thatkindofgirl.shop/7psnm3t5dj

Opal

2019

"Our flight leaves in an hour. Are you finished at the hospital yet?" Fox's text read. I knew he wouldn't like the answer, so I tucked the phone back into my pocket without a reply. He said I needed to get away from this place or it would consume me. I had been swirling in a vortex, fracturing into microparticles of myself for so long I no longer realized I was sinking. Like debris in an oceanic garbage patch, I was floating through my life, indifferent to rescue or destruction. Fox wanted to be the one to pluck me out of the spiral. He wanted us to go north and change the scenery. I had no interest in finding myself on the side of a mountain.

"My mother needs me," I protested.

"Your mother needs you to be well."

"The children need me."

"The children have your mother."

"The hospital can't function without me," I persisted.

"The hospital should get used to functioning without you," he replied. "Why is this job so important to you, anyway?"

"This job *is* me," I replied. "Who am I if I'm not the one saving these people?"

I could have been at the airport right now. Tom offered to take the pager, but I didn't let him. I didn't want to be like Karen—everyone hated Karen. Then, Mr. Harris showed up with chest pain. I still wasn't worried. Chest pain patients were always quick. This one had to be fast—I had a husband and an airplane waiting for me.

Inside Ocean Hospital, the seasons never changed. If you peer out the small window in the doctor's charting room, you can glimpse the pounding rain, blazing sun, and, every so often, palm trees whipping in the winds of a tropical storm. Inside, it was always 72 degrees, fluorescent sunshine with no chance of rain. The charting room was a sparsely furnished rectangle tucked behind the ICU. From the window, the view was mostly of a parking lot. The clock no longer kept time, and a tiny bonsai tree was the only decoration on the windowsill. In contrast, someone designed the common areas of Ocean Hospital to look like a hotel. They must have hired a designer because someone thought to install linoleum floors that mimicked hardwood like the floors at the high-end Walmarts. Those floors had seen things–vomit, blood spatter, or worse. It all wiped away. With a little Lysol and a Starbucks next to the gift shop, violà!, Hotel Ocean Hospital. Framed artwork of sailboats, beaches, sunsets, or palm trees lined the walls in the corridors between wards. Isabelle Aberdeen herself had designed the entire remodel when Ronald Aberdeen took over the company.

I encountered Mr. Harris in a private patient room. Decorative cabinets concealed oxygen and suction lines around the bed, and a 54-inch television hung on the opposite wall. Mr. Harris was a handsome forty-something man with the most mundane chest pain. He was a talker. I kept track, and I'm pretty sure he hadn't come up for air in the last twenty minutes.

I listened intently to his description of the jalapeño cheese sauce that rarely caused this type of heartburn. The longer he talked, the more I became distracted by some sort of rock in my shoe. How did it get there, and would I get it out soon? I needed that rock out of my shoe before I could dash to catch a plane. I glanced at the clock and then over at him lying in his hospital bed. He was describing the new cycling group he had joined. I tried to judge how he would react if I took my shoe off and shook it out while he finished his story.

"You can go ahead and order a CAT scan of my belly while I'm here," he was saying. "And my primary care doctor wanted me to have some blood work. I'll just have you get that, too. You can call him and figure out which labs he wanted—-"

The rock must have been sharp. I think it was actually piercing the skin on the bottom of my foot. I imagined the tiny prick of blood staining the sole of my shoe. Not wanting to ruin my twenty-dollar pair of flats, I bent over, still locking eyes with my man, and whisked the shoe from my foot. The pungent scent of a ten-hour day in twenty-dollar flats reminded me why I should generally try to keep my shoes on while in patients' rooms.

"Sir," I interrupted. "You're here with chest pain. We may not need to scan your belly right now." I admonished him gently. The patients don't like it when you're mean. Being mean puts you at risk of getting a low Press Ganey score. He had gotten out of the bed and was changing into a hospital gown. Next, he would unpack toiletries from a bag he had brought with him and line them up on a small table next to his bed.

"No, doctor," the man persisted. "Wait, you are the doctor, right?" He squinted at me as I held my shoe. Balancing on one foot, I lifted my unkempt toes above the floor. "Who are you, again?"

"Opal Collins," I replied.

Who was I? If he had asked that question before this crazy life, I would have answered that I had come from the earth itself. Native blood coursed through my veins. I came into the world with strong, angular features that betrayed my delicate constitution. My mother named me Opal in honor of the precious mineral, expecting I would shine. But just as the opalescent gem is built upon the earth's natural faults, I would carve my path through a series of failures to reach this venerable state in a designer hospital room.

"Anyway," continued Mr. Harris, "I'm going to need you to order that CAT scan. Also, my sleeping pill. And I'll need a refill prescription for the sleeping pills when I leave tomorrow, Dr... uh,"

"Collins," I supplied. "Look, Mr. Harris, you came in with chest pain, but you want a CAT scan of your belly and a prescription for sleeping pills?" I asked, slipping the shoe back on my foot.

"Well, you're the doctor. I just thought everything was about Press Ganey scores now." The forty-something man in the bed took a deep breath and launched back into his story. Just then, the loudspeaker crackled on at the same time as my pager began a frantic BEEP! BEEP! BEEP! BEEP! The operator's voice bellowed overhead, "Code Blue, 5A2. Code Blue, 5A2."

I cut off my man. "Mr... uh, Harris," I said, pointing at the voice coming from the ceiling. "That's me. Grab a magazine or something because I won't be back for a while."

About the Author

Jacey Bici writes Women's Fiction with a humorous twist. When she's not saving the world with Dad Jokes, you can find her in the Emergency Room of a Veterans hospital where she works as a doctor. She is honored to be immersed in genuine stories from real-life heroes.

Acknowledgments

Thank you to my readers who make it possible for me to share my work and continue to create new stories.

Thank you to my husband, Brian, for believing in my dream. Without your support, my stories would be dust on a shelf.

Thanks to my editor, Ali Bumbarger for giving me the tools to get this published in 2025 instead of 2035 and your sister A.N. Deeb for generously sharing your wealth of knowledge on publishing.

Thanks to Pam Hines for patiently growing me into a better writer.

Thank you to the many hundreds of patients who inspire me with your own stories.

www.ingramcontent.com/pod-product-compliance
Lightning Source LLC
LaVergne TN
LVHW051019080826
845145LV00009B/2699

* 9 7 8 1 9 6 9 1 6 0 0 5 9 *